This
Whitaker Playhouse
Book Belongs To:

In Him was life; and the life was the light of men.

John 1:4

The Story of Christmas
www.philsmouse.com
ISBN: 978-1-64123-687-4

Whitaker House
1030 Hunt Valley Circle
New Kensington, PA 15068
www.whitakerhouse.com

1 2 3 4 5 6 7 8 9 10 11 W 28 27 26 25 24 23 22 21

The Story of Christmas

A note to Parents...

Your word is a lamp to my feet, and a light to my path. Psalm 119:105

If you love the wonderful, rollicking rhythm and rhyme of the classic picture books you read as a child and want to bring that same sense of joy to your children, you're in the right place.

Learning, understanding, and living God's Word is a journey that lasts a lifetime. And that journey starts by reading God's Word. Every tiny heart on the face of this earth is trying to find its way home to Jesus. And God's eternal promise to our precious little lambs is that they will find Him—when we take the time to show them how and where look.

Jesus wants us to be His—one hundred percent. And the most important thing is not what we say or do, or even who we reach. The most important thing is the relationship we cultivate with Him.

That deep spiritual connection isn't only for adults. The truths you share with your children from God's Word will stay with them for the rest of their lives. This delightful, child-friendly Bible story is a perfect way to introduce those precious little ones to the joy of a heart filled with Jesus and the knowledge of God's Word.

Phil A. Smouse

Behold, I bring you
good tidings of great joy,
which shall be to all people.

Luke 2:10

We're getting close...

It's almost here!

My very favorite time of year!

The eggs are nogged.
The halls are decked.
The not-too-naughty lists are checked.

The bells are jingling, *"Ho-ho-ho!"*
We're dashing through the sparkling snow!

But while the shepherds watch their flocks,
and fill their cozy Christmas socks
with songs of joy and yuletide cheer,
a shining star sings, *"Do you hear?"*

A star-song soft like falling snow.
A song of joy from long ago,
that fills the dark with holy light,
and shines out on this silent night.

A night alive with heaven-sights,
as strings of joyful, dancing lights
proclaim from every house and tree,
I once was blind but now I see!

And in those homes,
hearts burst with joy,
unwrapping boxes,
filled with toys!

Like gifts from heaven.
Works of art.
The beauty of our Father's heart.

For Christ is with us
on this night
to fill His world
with holy light.

As every silent star proclaims,
Joy to the world
He came to save!

In every Christmas song we sing,
In everyone and *everything*.
In every cookie, pie and sweet.
In every chocolate covered treat.

In every hug
and tummy ache!
In every stockinged step we take.
Lord let us be a holy light,
that shines out on this silent night.

For unto us a child is born,
and on that wintery Christmas morn',
the gift of heaven, softly laid,
is God with us. . .

To seek and save!

O come! O come!
Make all things new.
Our hearts and homes make room for you.
Jesus with us. All is well.

The gift of God...

Emmanuel!

And there were in the same country
shepherds abiding in the field,
keeping watch over their flock by night.

And, lo, the angel of the Lord came upon them,
and the glory of the Lord shone round about them:
and they were sore afraid.

And the angel said to them, Fear not:
for, behold, I bring you good tidings of great joy,
which shall be to all people.

For to you is born this day
in the city of David a Savior,
which is Christ the Lord.

Luke 2:8-11

There's still more fun from Whitaker Playhouse.

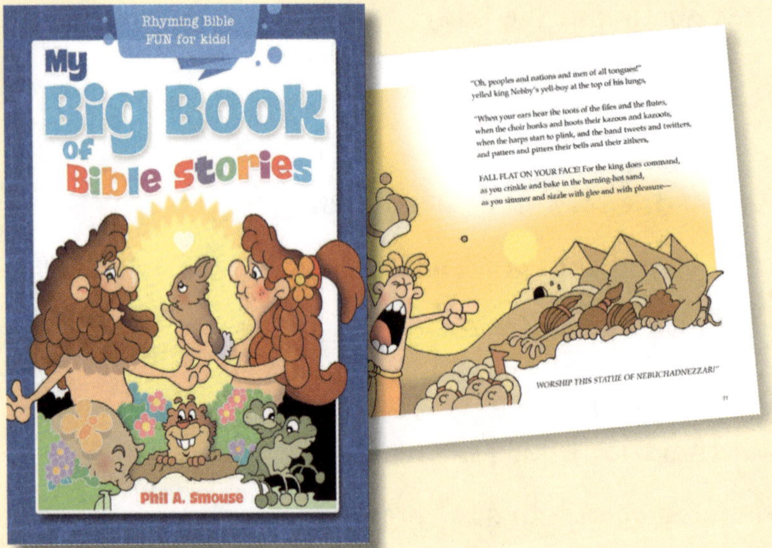

My Big Book of Bible Stories
978-1-64123-548-8

From award-winning author and illustrator Phil A. Smouse, *My Big Book of Bible Stories* features seventeen favorite Bible stories told in hilarious rhymes, with bright, full-color illustrations. These clever retellings of key Scriptures from the Old and New Testaments include the stories of creation, Adam and Eve, Jonah, the Good Samaritan, Jesus and Nicodemus, Peter, and more. Parents will enjoy reading *My Big Book of Bible Stories* to their preschool children, while young readers will delight in the whimsical story-telling and artwork.

My Big Book of Bible People, Places, and Things
978-1-64123-549-5

This brand-new Bible dictionary for kids features 750 entries with witty, age-appropriate text and colorful illustrations from award-winning author and illustrator Phil A. Smouse. *My Big Book of Bible People, Places, and Things* explains important terms in simple ways that young readers can easily grasp, while the full-color illustrations enhance your child's learning. With such entries as "Alleluia," "Book of Life," "Mary and Martha," and "Walking on Water," this book provides an important head start to scriptural literacy.

Bible ABCs 978-1-64123-428-3

Noah's Animals 978-1-64123-429-0

Away in a Manger 978-1-64123-527-3

Bible Activities 978-1-64123-430-6

Bible 123s 978-1-64123-427-6

Merry Christmas 978-1-64123-528-0

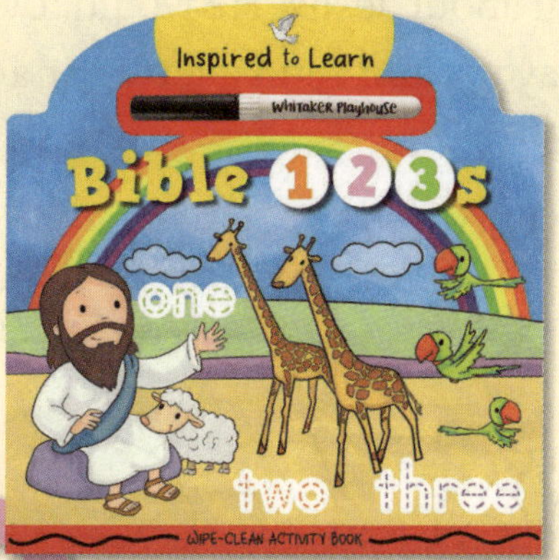

Wipe-Clean Activity Books

The *Inspired to Learn* series from Whitaker Playhouse is a perfect way for parents to share God's love with children while also introducing early learning concepts in a fun, interactive way.

These durable, wipe-clean books will provide hours of entertainment as children learn counting, the alphabet, color and shape recognition, drawing, spotting differences, and more. Parents will delight in their little one's progress as they enjoy the creative exercises.

Write to Phil A. Smouse

Once upon a time, Phil A. Smouse wanted to be a scientist.

But scientists don't get wonderful letters and pictures from friends like you. So Phil decided to draw and color instead! He and his wife live in sunny Lancaster, Pennsylvania. They have two married children, a granddaughter, and a goofy dog they love with all their heart.

Phil loves to tell kids like you all about Jesus. He would love to hear from you today! So get out your markers and crayons and send a letter or a picture to:

Phil A. Smouse
Whitaker House
1030 Hunt Valley Circle
New Kensington, PA 15068

Or visit his website at www.philsmouse.com
and send him an e-mail at: phil@philsmouse.com